P

Toad was hot. Toad was tired. But Toad was happy. At last he was coming home to Farthing Wood.

He hopped slowly, dragging his tired legs on the rough ground. "If I can just keep going a little longer —" he panted. "I'll soon be home."

Suddenly, a shadow fell across him. Toad heard a grinding noise of gears shifting, then a giant metal claw scooped him up!

"Help!" Toad shouted frantically. "Help! Put me down!"

The claw turned over, and tipped Toad out. A pile of earth and stones fell on top of him.

Kestrel swooped down to perch beside Owl.

"Have you heard?" she said. "They're filling in the pond!"

Owl gasped. Badger groaned. Weasel tried to look cheerful.

"At least we've still got the stream," she pointed out.

"But it's only a muddy trickle now," said Badger gloomily. "Come and see."

Some hedgehogs and rabbits were trying to drink at the few remaining puddles.

Suddenly, they squeaked with fright. Fox had arrived.

"This is a crisis," he said. "Make no mistake. We can't live without water."

"What can we do?" said everyone together.

Everyone scurried away to spread the news.

"An Assembly! At midnight!" called the squirrels in the treetops.

"In Badger's set!" squeaked the shrews in the long grass.

"We've forgotten our snakey friend, Adder," said Weasel with a shudder.

"Find her then," said Badger, "but warn her to behave."

As night fell, Badger got to work. Clods of earth flew out of his set.

"Watch out!" said Weasel, passing by.

Badger came up blinking.

"Sorry," he said. "I'm trying to make more room down here. Why don't you fetch some glow worms? We're going to need their light."

Everyone else followed.

"Not lassst, am I?" said Adder, at the end of the line.

"Yes, you are," said Badger, "and Adder, don't eat the glow worms!"

"Of courssse I won't!" said Adder, but she did look disappointed.

When all of the animals had settled down,
Badger cleared his throat.

"Now listen, everyone," he began.

"Wait," said Weasel. "Where's Mole?"

There was a sudden scrabbling noise
overhead, and a crack appeared in the roof
of the set, then one paw, and then another.

"Sorry I'm late, everyone," said Mole in a small voice.

Fox stepped forward. "Animals," he said, "we're in great danger. Our wood is being destroyed and our pond has gone. Once it was home to forty-seven toads. The last one left months ago, and never returned..."

Outside, in the darkness of Farthing Wood, something was moving. Toad, bruised and dazed, had managed at last to dig his way out of the pile of earth on top of him.

"I'm still alive!" he croaked. "And I'm home! At least, I think I am. But where is everyone?" Toad looked round.

In the moonlight he saw Farthing Wood.
It looked smaller than he remembered.

"I'm coming, mateys," he called, painfully
hopping along. "Toad's here! Toad's back!
I'm coming!"

Suddenly, he felt the soft earth give way
beneath him. He was falling again, down
and down into the ground!

21

He nearly landed right on Weasel's tail.

"Well, bless my soul, it's that daft Toad," sniffed Owl. "I thought you were gone for good."

"So did I," said Toad, smiling round at all his friends.

"Where have you been all this time, Toad?" asked Rabbit.

"Where haven't I been, more like," said Toad. "Caught in a jam jar, I was, and carried far away by a nasty human child. But I bided my time, and escaped. I've been travelling for months. Horrible, it was. 'I must get back to my mateys,' I kept thinking. 'I must get back to my pond.'"

There was an awkward silence.

"The pond isss gone," said Adder. "Filled in."

"What?" gasped Toad. "No! It isn't true!"
Tears trickled out of his large, staring eyes.

"I'm sorry, Toad," said Fox, "but you might
as well know the truth. Farthing Wood is
being destroyed. We've got to leave. That's
why we've called an Assembly."

24

He turned to the birds. "Can you help us?
You travel far and wide. Is there another
pond nearby?"

Pheasant shook his head. "My wife and I
never venture out of the wood," he said.
"We might be, er—"

"Shot," said Hen Pheasant bluntly.

"I know a place where we could go," said Toad quietly. "It's a perfect place. No humans anywhere. Only animals allowed."

"Only animals?" everyone echoed in disbelief. "Where? Tell us where!"

"It's called White Deer Park," said Toad. "It's a nature reserve. It's a terribly long journey, but I could lead you there."

Fox looked at Badger. Badger nodded.

"We have no choice," said Fox. "White Deer Park it must be. But first..." He looked round at the ring of faces.

"We must take the Ancient Woodland Vow. We must all promise to help one another and..." Now he looked particularly at Adder, Weasel and Owl. "... *not* to eat each other."

Everyone started talking at once.

"We must have a leader," said Badger. "Someone brave, and cunning, and strong."

"Fox! Fox!" the animals shouted.

"Thank you," said Fox. "Here's my first order. Rest and eat for one more day. We'll start our journey tomorrow at midnight."

The animals agreed and said goodnight.

Badger gazed around his set.

"My home sweet home," he whispered sadly. "Farewell, Farthing Wood."